# THE SCARRED AMISH BRIDE

## AMISH ROMANCE

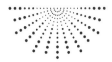

## SARAH MILLER

JOIN MY NEWSLETTER

# CHAPTER ONE

*But you are a chosen people, a royal priesthood, a holy
nation, God's special possession, that you may declare
the praises of him who called you out of darkness into
his wonderful light.*

1 Peter 2:9

Gloria completed the stitching on one part
of her quilt. Admiring the beautiful and
intricate work she sat back to admire it
with the crackle of the fire in the background. It was
a fairly simple quilt, except for the different patterns
in the middle.

This commission had been for a baby quilt with a pink and white checkered background. Each checkered area had a picture of a baby animal in the middle. There were likenesses of baby bunny rabbits, bears, ducks, chicks, deer, horses, and owls. She knew that this was a great learning tool for mothers when they were teaching their children different animals, as well as how to read at times. However, the main reason that she enjoyed making quilts with animals on them was because she had a great love for them, but she was never allowed to have a pet of her own. This was the closest thing she ever had to one.

Now that it was complete, she folded it neatly and put it down. She would deliver it to its new home tomorrow. Then she picked up the other quilt that she had been working on. It was her favorite and she was secretly thinking of keeping it for herself. It was a basic checkerboard quilt pattern with a golden Labrador stitched throughout the piece. This could be the dog she never had. She smiled to herself thinking about that.

There was a loud knock on the door and her *daed* got up from his chair to answer it. He set his Bible down on the table next to him.

"*Gut* evening, Bishop Amos. Please come in." Her *daed* opened the door and let him inside the house.

"*Gut* evening everyone," Amos answered.

"Hello Bishop," Gloria said as her hand automatically went up to the left side of her face to cover it. Her face was scarred on the left side from a fire when she was a little girl. She knew that it was hidden from sight, but it was such a reflex for her to cover it from embarrassment that her hand went up to it all the time. She wasn't really in the mood to entertain company tonight and dropping her head she went back to her stitching.

Her *daed* led Amos into the living room and offered him a seat on the sofa. Her *mamm* brought out some *kaffe* and set it on the living room table.

"*Denke*," Amos said as he poured himself a cup.

"What brings you here tonight Bishop?" her *daed* asked.

Amos ran his fingers through his beard, which indicated that he was thinking. "I came here today because I wanted to check up on all of you. I haven't seen you in a while and I have been hearing good things about Gloria's quilt making," he said.

She wondered if he knew that she was listening to their conversation. She didn't utter a word and kept on stitching and paying attention to the conversation right in front of her.

"Things have been doing quite well for us, and for Gloria's business. Her quilts have been getting a lot of attention lately. And, we can say that we are humbly proud of her," her *daed* said.

His words made her smile. He had always been a fan of her craftsmanship and referred people to her when they were interested in having an authentic quilt made.

"That is *gut*," The Bishop responded. "It is always *gut* to hear that our gifts are being put to *gut* use."

Gloria stopped listening to the conversation and gave all of her attention to her work. The fire crackled in the background and she sighed in comfort. Working into the dead of night on something she loved was one of her favorite past times. She started humming to herself and was vaguely listening to what was going on around her. The voices became background noise until she heard someone mention the word marriage a couple of times.

She sat up in her chair and opened up her ears to the conversation. Yet, the conversation seemed to change the moment she did that. She didn't hear anyone referring to her or to the topic of marriage again. But, it still stuck in her head. Gloria was twenty-seven years old and she was unmarried. She still lived with her parents and helped take care of her siblings. She really loved her life, but she was afraid of marriage. After the fire left her with a scar on her face, she could never think about a man loving her for her beauty. She knew that would never be the case. No man would ever love her when they had to look at the ugliness on her face. She knew that she wasn't marriage material, which did make her sad, but she had gotten used to it.

Bishop Amos excused himself for the evening to go home to his *fraa*. Gloria continued to lose herself in her work and soon forgot about what was said earlier and before she knew it, it was time to go to bed. Gloria started packing up her work for the night and put everything away in its proper place. She knew this was going to be the first project that she picked up in the morning.

Gloria went up to the loft and laid down. She knew that she had a big day ahead of her tomorrow. She needed to finish a couple of quilts for some clients, but she couldn't get the conversation she overheard out of her head. *Were they really talking about her? Were they trying to arrange a marriage behind her back?* The thought alone scared her because she should be a part of that discussion. She had every reason to discuss with her parents her fear about marriage and why it hadn't interested her in all of these years. She just hoped that they would listen and respect her wishes. This was her choice after all.

# CHAPTER TWO

*Wives, in the same way submit yourselves to your own husbands so that, if any of them do not believe the word, they may be won over without words by the behavior of their wives...*

*1 Peter 3*

Gloria walked into service with her parents and sat down next to her *mamm*. She felt all jittery today and could not get comfortable. She kept moving around the bench, but every part of her body just wanted to get outside and away from the scrutiny.

"What is the matter with you?" her *mamm* asked her.

Gloria was still thinking about what happened the previous night. She couldn't get the thought of an arranged marriage out of her mind. "Are you sure that you two weren't discussing an arranged marriage with the Bishop about me last night?" she asked again.

"The conversation we had last night was not about you. Can we drop this? The service is about to start, and I do not want to be rude to everyone else in here." Her *mamm* glared at her.

Gloria was still not convinced but she tried to get into the spirit of the service, only now she was too self-conscious. She kept looking around to make sure that no one was looking at her, women or men. She was usually self-conscious about her scar, but now she was worried that people were watching her because of the conversation.

She had no idea if anyone else knew what was really going on. Maybe it was her brother that was part of this arranged marriage situation. She started to scoot down lower on the bench to make herself more inconspicuous, and she leaned her hand on her face to cover her scar as well.

She was tired of watching people's eyes as they always moved to look at it. She told herself to breathe because the service would be over soon, and she would be able to go back home where it was safe and away from everyone.

Matthew sat down right behind Gloria's *daed*. Butterflies danced in his stomach every time he thought about her. He carefully searched for her in the crowd because he didn't want other people seeing him watching her. The whole idea was uncomfortable in itself. His breath caught as he spotted her in her blue dress sitting in one of the middle pews with her family. She had her left hand resting on her face. Whenever she moved, her hand moved with it like it was a fixture on her face.

He had noticed Gloria a couple of months ago when the idea of marriage had actually come into his head. He had never really thought of it before. But, now that his parents were gone, he had time in his life to think about his future and not have to worry about taking care of them. He knew that they would be very proud of him to keep the family name going, and that was what he intended to do. Now, he just needed to find a wife and that was where Gloria came in.

He had always liked Gloria. She was a nice girl and was never mean to him. He also hated how all the other boys treated her when they were growing up. He was still surprised that someone like her would not be married at her age, for she was beautiful.

He saw her fidgeting in her seat and he wondered what kind of person she was. What kind of things she thought? And he realized that he wanted to know more about her. He wanted to know what made her eyes light up and what made her smile. He wanted to know what excited her and what things she was passionate about. He continued to watch her during the entire service and how she responded to certain things that the Bishop said. When the service was over he decided to go and ask Gloria if he could drive her home.

Everyone started to congregate outside of the service hall and Matthew walked behind Gloria's *daed* knowing that his family would find their way to him. This was when he would make his move.

"Oh, there you are," Gloria said to her *daed* with the rest of her family behind her. Though normally they would stay for a meal and a get together, today they all decided to leave and head home for some family time.

Matthew tried to muster up his courage to ask Gloria, but when he reached around to tap her shoulder something inside him stopped him from asking her. He didn't know if it was fear or what? He had spent most of his life taking care of his parent's farm and then taking care of his ailing daed. He was a very strong person, but he started to feel weak whenever he was around her. He couldn't even open his mouth to say hi.

"Can I help you son?" Thomas asked him.

Matthew's cheeks started to get red in embarrassment when everyone looked in his direction. He told himself that he needed to say this now, for if he didn't he wouldn't be able to say it at all.

"Oh, Matthew. How have you been?" Sarah, Gloria's *mamm* asked him.

"I am *gut*," he responded, which sparked up a conversation between him and Gloria's parents. He noticed her scowling at him from the other side of the room and it killed his resolve.

"How are things at the farm?" Thomas asked him.

"They are doing well. Business has been improving since I have been able to spend more of my time working. It was hard to take care of the business and my *daed* when he was sick, and I know that there was quite some time where the business was not my first priority," he answered.

Thomas nodded in response.

"It is nice to have something to keep your mind off of things isn't it?" Sarah asked.

Matthew nodded and then turned toward Gloria. He cleared his throat and decided to just go for it. What was the worst thing that could happen?

"Gloria, I was wondering if you would be so kind as to let me take you home today?" he asked. He could feel his legs shaking.

Gloria glared at him in response to his question, which made him sweat even more. He didn't understand what was taking so long. The wait was making him feel miserable.

# CHAPTER THREE

*Finally, all of you, be like-minded, be sympathetic,*
*love one another, be compassionate and humble*
*1 Peter 3:8*

**\* \* \***

Gloria saw him from the other side of the room watching her. It made her even more uncomfortable than before. Why would someone that handsome and eligible for marriage be interested in her? She knew that she was not considered marriageable. She looked down at her overweight, unattractive body and as the scar on her face burned with embarrassment, she started to get angry. There was no way that he was taking notice of her beauty.

Shaking her head, she tried to focus her attention on the Bishop's sermon, but she could feel his eyes staring through the back of her head and it started to aggravate her even more. What did this man want with her? Gloria started thinking about when they were kids. Matthew was actually kind of nice to her when the other kids bullied her and called her names, especially after her face was scarred. He didn't go out of his way to say nice things to her, but he was never mean to her either.

She remembered one day at the playground. *Matthew was running around with some of his other friends who stopped and looked at her when she left the bathroom. They started to tease her and call her names. Gloria tried to get away from them, but they were relentless. Matthew ran faster than the other boys and he almost caught up with her. She tried to outrun him, but he caught up with her. She stopped dead in her tracks, afraid that he was going to do something. He turned toward the other boys and stood in front of her. He told them all to leave her alone. She had done nothing to them and they should respect her and treat her nicely. Backed down by his courage, the boys shook their heads and ran off to create mischief somewhere else. Matthew stayed and looked her right in the face.*

*"They shouldn't bother you again," he said before he ran off to join them.*

*Gloria didn't know how to react to what just happened. No one had ever been that nice to her before and for no reason either. She smiled as she let her body relax, and she enjoyed her first recess without having to find a place to hide but out there in the open.*

A smile formed on her face as she remembered the day that Matthew had protected her from the bullies in her class. However, that was one of the only times that she could remember their paths crossing. She couldn't remember another time that the two of them spoke since then, maybe some just in passing. The thought confounded her, and she felt the anger forming again. Her mother must have noticed her being antsy because she gave her a look. Gloria faced forward and tried to ignore the man watching her from the other room.

When the service was over, Gloria got up real fast

and made a beeline for her *daed*. The rest of her family ran behind her. They probably questioned what was really going on with her, but she couldn't stay there any longer. She needed to get away from the bench and the prying eyes that were burning into the back of her head.

"Can I help you son?" her *daed* asked.

Gloria pushed her body against the wall when her *daed* addressed Matthew. How did he get all the way over here so fast? She watched his face redden in embarrassment when in response to her *daed's* question.

Her parents continued to have a conversation with Matthew, asking him about his farm and his life after his parents passing. It all started to click inside Gloria's head. Her parents had orchestrated this entire operation. They made sure that they would run into him after service to question him in front of her. They must think that she was really stupid.

She leaned closer to the back wall. Maybe if she continued to push herself she could disappear into the wall altogether and she wouldn't have to face the embarrassment of listening to them talk about the possibility of what the rest of her life would be like.

Matthew kept looking in her direction and smiling. She glared back at him hoping that might scare him away from her. But he didn't even notice. He just went back to talking to her parents. After a few more minutes of him talking she decided that she was going to get out of the service hall faster, so that he couldn't approach her. She moved her back away from the wall and slowly started to inch toward the door hoping that she was unnoticed.

"Where are you going Gloria?" her mother asked.

Gloria turned and faced her parents. They both were looking at her wondering why she had decided to leave so rudely. She really had no answer to give them.

"I needed to use the restroom," she said saving face.

Matthew spoke before she could leave the room, now that she made her excuse.

"Gloria, I was wondering if you would be so kind as to let me take you home today?"

There it was; the question that she had been trying

to avoid the entire time. At that exact moment, she knew that her parents had put him up to this and she was not going to be any part of it. She had every right to choose if she wanted to get married or not and she chose not to.

"Thank you so much for the kind offer, but at this time I am not interested in any type of offer for marriage," she rebuffed.

Then she turned and headed toward the bathroom leaving them all behind with her response ringing in their ears. They thought that they were so conniving, but she had caught onto them last night when they had broached the subject of marriage with the Bishop. She had no idea why they had lied to her and it hurt.

## CHAPTER FOUR

*12 Dear friends, do not be surprised at the fiery ordeal
that has come on you to test you, as though something
strange were happening to you. 13 But
rejoice inasmuch as you participate in the sufferings
of Christ, so that you may be overjoyed when his glory
is revealed. 14 If you are insulted because of the name
of Christ, you are blessed, for the Spirit of glory and of
God rests on you.*

*1 Peter 4:12-14*

\* \* \*

"Thank you so much for the kind offer,
but at this time I am not interested in
any type of offer for marriage," she rebuffed him.

The answer rang in his ears over and over again. What was wrong with her? There was no thought of marriage. Why wasn't she interested in riding home with him? They didn't even know if they would work together or have anything in common. He had no idea why she was pushing that part of herself away.

He pulled the horse and buggy around the side of the barn and unhitched the horse and dealt with him automatically. Once finished he walked into his *haus* aimlessly. He really didn't know what to think or feel at this moment. His entire life he felt that *Gott* had left Gloria without a husband because they were supposed to be together. She was waiting for him, but maybe he was actually wrong about that. Maybe Matthew wasn't supposed to have a family.

Matthew sat down at the kitchen table and rubbed his hands together. He felt at such a loss right now. He knew what he wanted, but his follow-through did not go as planned.

"*Gott,* I don't know what to do anymore," he said as he bowed his head in prayer. "I don't know what you have planned for my life, but I do know one thing, I do not want to be alone anymore. I have spent my life taking care of my family and their farm, and now

I would like to have a family of my own. I want a marriage. I want a *fraa* and my own *kinner*," he said.

When he finished his prayer, the image of Gloria popped into his mind. He thought about her face when she was listening to the Bishop during service and how her eyes lit up when she smiled. Matthew knew that he had to trust *Gott* in this matter and whatever happened, happened. He knew that he had no more control in this situation than he had when he lost his ailing father.

For the next two weeks, he went about his business and continued to take care of the farm and with his life. He kept his schedule every day and it was easy to keep his mind off of things when he wanted to. The work was a steady distraction from Gloria during the day, but when he was lying in bed alone every night he couldn't keep her off of his mind. He tried a lot of different things, but something always led back to her.

One night he tried thinking about other eligible girls that he could take to service, but they never stirred anything inside of him unlike when he thought of Gloria. He sighed in frustration and rolled over in bed.

I know what I'll do. I'm going to go and talk to the Bishop tomorrow before service. He might have some advice for me, he thought to himself. This made him feel a little bit more comfortable and he got himself a good night's rest.

"Come in," Amos said. A knock on the door startled him and brought him out of his head. He was preparing for the service later on this morning.

Matthew stuck his head in the door and walked into the room.

*Gut* morning Bishop. I was wondering if you had a few moments to spare? I would like to speak to you about something," Matthew said.

Amos gestured for the young man to sit down.

"What did you need to talk to me about?" Amos asked.

Matthew sat up in his chair. "I have been having a difficult time as of late. I know that I want to marry, but the girl that I'm interested in doesn't seem to be interested in me. I can't get her off of my mind and there are no other girls that strike my attention. I don't know what to do Amos. I have prayed on it," he said.

"I think you need to give this young woman some time. If she knows that you have taken a liking to her it might have caught her off guard and made her feel uncomfortable. Just trust in the plan that *Gott* has for your life and know that he is steering you in the right direction. You don't ever have to worry because he will get you there." Amos smiled and nodded his head making his long grey beard nod with him.

This made Matthew think long and hard. It was true. Things were going to happen the way that He wanted them to and there was nothing that Matthew or Gloria could do about it.

"Thank you for your wise words. I will trust in knowing that He will lead me to the path that I am going to take. I just get a little frustrated and impatient at times," Matthew said.

"I know. It can be hard going along with His wishes, especially when we do not know what they are. This is why you have to continue to pray until He reveals His plans to you. This might be something that you would like to think about when you are in service today," Amos said.

"It did very much. *Denke* for your wise words. I will reflect on this when I am in service today." Matthew walked out of the Bishop's office feeling a little more confident that he was making the right choice by waiting for *Gott* to reveal His plan to him. He would be patient and make sure that he didn't try to force his own agenda.

The service hall opened, and he went to find a seat. He sighed knowing that he would have peace of mind because he made the right decision. Taking a relaxing breath he looked around the room to see who else had come to service today. As always, most of the district was there and he nodded at some familiar faces and waved or said hi to people as they passed by. The bishop's talk had really helped, he had faith that things were going to turn out just right.

CHAPTER FIVE

*To the elders among you, I appeal as a fellow
elder and a witness of Christ's sufferings who also
will share in the glory to be revealed: 2 Be shepherds
of God's flock that is under your care, watching over
them—not because you must, but because you are
willing, as God wants you to be; not pursuing
dishonest gain, but eager to serve; 3 not lording it over
those entrusted to you, but being examples to
the flock.*
*1 Peter 5: 5-3*

\* \* \*

*G*loria threw down the quilt. She had been irritated all week. All she has overheard was her parents talking about the wedding and it has started to get to her. She didn't want to get married because she had too. At this point, she didn't want to get married at all. She just wanted to be content and to go on with her life enjoying her quilting and making her customers happy.

"Why do you continue to have a scowl on your face? You have had one the entire week?" her sister Melissa asked her.

"You wouldn't understand if I told you. You have always been a pretty girl, and no one has ever made fun of you because of the way that you have looked," Gloria said in response.

"Melissa, go and finish your chores. We need to talk to Gloria," her *daed* said, an understanding smile on his face.

Melissa left the room and stuck her tongue out at Gloria in fun just before she closed the door. It brought a smile to Gloria's face and a touch of joy to her heart. Melissa had never judged her and would be there if she needed to talk.

"Gloria, you have always been a *gut* example to your sister. But, this week you have been someone very angry and irritable. This is not the *dochder* that we are used to. What is going on with you?"

Gloria bit back the sigh as she turned. Her *mamm* was there now and she stared at her parents in disbelief. Did they really not understand what was going on? Did they not see what they had done?

"I have been happy for a really long time. I enjoy my life here, especially my quilting. Why would you want to take that away from me?" Gloria asked, feeling herself close to tears.

"What do you mean?" her *daed* asked.

Gloria felt a spark of anger which always made her scar burn. They were still going to hide this arranged marriage they had been whispering about all week. "Why would you want to do something to ruin my life?" she asked.

"We don't know what you're talking about, young lady." Her *daed* shook his head and looked genuinely perplexed.

The agitation was building in Gloria's chest. She

didn't understand why they were playing games with her. "I will not be forced to marry a man that I do not love. I will not marry Matthew, and I definitely will not marry for pity," she spat out the words and felt awful for being so angry.

Both of her parents looked at her like she was crazy.

"We don't know what you're talking about," her *mamm* said. "No one is trying to marry you off. What kind of parents do you think we are? We have never even broached the subject of marriage with you. And, if we were thinking about helping you get married, we would have talked to you about it first," she said with conviction.

Gloria looked her *mamm* in the face. She could never remember one time when that woman lied to her about anything. But, for some reason she couldn't find it in herself to trust her now. They had had a conversation with the Bishop the other night about marriage and whenever she asked about it they brushed the subject off. This made her think that they were hiding something.

"You both were talking about marriage the other night when the Bishop was here. Whenever I ask you about it, you tell me that the conversation wasn't about me, but you never tell me what the conversation was actually about. So, how am I supposed to believe you two are not conspiring about me behind my back when you cannot give me a detailed answer? You are keeping something from me and if you are going to continue to hide it from me, what do you expect me to believe?" she asked them.

Her *daed* put his head in his hands and shook it.

"If we tell you that our conversation is not about you, you do not need to question us. *Jah*, we might not have given you all of the information when you asked the question, but that doesn't mean that we are lying. It just means that we do not think that we should tell you everything at that particular point in time. Do you understand me?"

Gloria nodded in response. Doubt still reared its ugly head in her mind, but what else could she do?

Her *mamm* sighed and her face relaxed.

"You know that I enjoy planning weddings and am always a part of them every chance I get," her *mamm* reminded her. "Well, this happens to be one of those chances. Your cousin Rebecca is getting married in a couple of months and she asked if we could help her plan her wedding. This was why Amos came over that night. He came to give us the news. That was all we were discussing. I do want to let you know that I would have loved to discuss your wedding with the Bishop. However, we have already come to terms with the fact that you might not ever get married. Whatever *Gott* has in store for your life, we will accept. You just need to trust and believe us." She came forward and took Gloria's hand squeezing it gently.

Gloria felt a little bit of guilt at her *mamm's* response. She was glad that the wedding they were planning happened to be her cousin's. But why did they have to keep that from her? Why couldn't they just tell her, so that she didn't think they were talking about her? They knew that she had been struggling with that conversation for weeks. Sometimes it felt like they didn't care about how they made her feel.

Marriage was a huge subject for Gloria because she had never thought it was an option for her. She had been teased for her scars most of her life, and she had no idea if there was anyone who had ever thought her beautiful, and that included her parents. That was why she knew that she would never be married. How could she ever be married to a man that couldn't look at her face with anything but horror. She wanted to be like the woman that was talked about in the Song of Solomon. She wanted to know what love like that felt like and she would never consider marrying a man that didn't look at her like she was the most beautiful woman in the world.

Yet this was just a childish dream and her logical mind knew it was pure folly.

# CHAPTER SIX

*And when the Chief Shepherd appears, you will*
*receive the crown of glory that will never fade away*
*1 Peter 5: 4*

\* \* \*

Gloria lay down in bed thinking about the conversation that she had with her parents. Though she hated it, she did feel a small twinge of jealousy that her cousin Rebecca would be enjoying her wedding day sometime soon. She knew that she should be happy for her, but she didn't understand why *Gott* had to lay this great burden on her shoulders.

Why did she have to survive a fire at a young age and then be scarred from it? She remembered how soft and smooth her skin was before the fire; before she was deformed. She was a normal child then, with normal friends. Once she was scarred, all of her friends started to slowly pull themselves away from her. That was one of the things that hurt the most. And then the bullying started. Tears started to form in the corner of her eyes the more she thought about it, the less she understood why *Gott* spared her that day.

So she prayed.

"Dear Gott. Please give me a sign of what I should do with my life. I thought I had it all figured out, but now I feel lost with the whole marriage talk. I had resigned myself to a life alone, but I know now, that is not really what I want. Could there be someone out there specifically meant for me?" she asked as she prayed. After she finished her prayers, she turned over and fell asleep.

The next morning, she woke feeling a little better. She had let go and now she would let Gott. When she came downstairs she found her *schweschder* helping her *mamm* make breakfast.

"Did you hear that Mrs. Thompson's golden Labrador has just had puppies this morning?" her Melissa said out loud, her voice full of excitement.

"Where did you hear that?" Gloria asked, her heart suddenly beat so fast and loud she thought they must hear.

"From Jabidah when he delivered some eggs this morning," Melissa said as she turned eggs on to plates with the already cooked bacon and tomatoes.

Gloria sat down at the table and ate breakfast with her family. She couldn't stop thinking about the puppies. After breakfast, she had to run a few errands in town and decided to take a walk since it was a nice day outside. She was going to pass by the Thompson's farm on the way to the store and couldn't resist having a look at the puppies. She walked up the walkway and knocked on the door.

"Hello Gloria," Mrs. Thompson said as she opened the door.

"Hello. I heard that your dog had puppies and I was hoping that you would let me see them?" she asked.

"Of course. Please come in," Mrs. Thompson opened

the door and let her in. Smiling all the time she led her into one of the back bedrooms where the puppies were being kept in.

Gloria walked in and was greeted by seven, eight-week-old puppies and their mother. She felt like she was in Heaven. She wanted to take every single one of those puppies' home with her. Of course, she knew that could never happen. Her parents would never allow her to have even one. The little bundles of golden joy jumped, yipped, and made snuffling noises. One in particular snuggled into her hands as she held it and Gloria knew that she was in love. Setting the puppy down she knew that it was time to leave, for this was so painful that she could feel tears prickling at the back of her eyes.

"Thank you for letting me see them. They are just perfect," she told Mrs. Thompson.

"You are very welcome dear," she said in response. Mrs. Thompson walked her out and she ran right into Matthew.

"Oh, excuse me," he said to Mrs. Thompson. "I heard that your dog just had a litter of puppies. I would like to see them if you have time."

Gloria walked out of the door and Mathew turned toward her. "Gloria. I wanted to apologize to you for what happened at service the other day. I never intended to insult you. I just wanted to get to know you better and drive you home that day. I promise it wasn't a proposition of marriage." He shrugged his shoulders and gave her a genuine smile.

That smile made her heart leap and she really didn't know what to make of what he said. Did she believe him or was this some kind of trick?

"Well *denke* you for your apology. But, why are you here today?" she asked him a little too harshly.

"It's been kind of lonely at the farmhouse since my parents passed away. I was thinking about getting a dog to help me pass the time," he said.

Gloria perked up when she heard that he was interested in taking one of the puppies' home. "Oh, that sounds *wunderbaar*, "she said in response.

"Would you like to help me choose one? It seems like you have already had a chance looking at them, and I would like to have your opinion if that is okay with you?" he asked.

Gloria nodded her head. "I would like that," she said following him back inside the house. She was really impressed with the fact that he had apologized to her. Maybe she had treated him badly that day at service because she was afraid of what her parents were trying to do to her. Now, that she was aware they were not planning her wedding, she could think a little more clearly.

Mrs. Thompson led them back inside the house and they followed her back to see the litter of puppies.

"I will leave you two to look," Mrs. Thompson said. "I'll just be in the kitchen, shout at me if you want a drink."

"Denke," Matthew said, and he went over to the whelping box come puppy pen and sat down on the floor.

The mother Labrador raised her head and wagged her tail. All the puppies were feeding and looking so cute Gloria felt her heart melt.

Though she was still nervous being around Matthew, now more than ever since he let her know what his intentions were that day, the sight of the puppies took over and she knelt down next to him while they finished their meal.

As she watched and laughed at their antics she snuck a look at him. He was very attractive with a strong jaw and thick hair. His eyes were kind and enraptured by the sight before her. Maybe she should give him a chance. After all, he did tell her that he didn't intend to offend her and that he wasn't proposing any type of marriage. However, he had wanted to get to know her better, and she didn't know how she felt about that. What were his motives to get to know her better? What was he really after? These thoughts played around in the back of her head while they waited for the puppies to finish eating. The sound of gentle muffled cries and grunts had both of them giggling.

Mrs. Thompson walked back in. "Okay, sorry for keeping you two waiting. Let me see, it looks like they have nearly finished so feel free to pick them up as you wish."

The Labrador mum jumped out of the box and walked up to Mrs. Thompson rubbing her head in her hand.

"They are the most precious little things. If we could keep all of them for ourselves, we would, but don't worry we can't. I'll take Daisy out for a moment and you take your time." She opened the door to let the dog out and left them to it.

CHAPTER SEVEN

*In the same way, you who are younger, submit
yourselves to your elders. All of you, clothe yourselves
with humility toward one another, because,
"God opposes the proud
but shows favor to the humble.
1 Peter 5:5*

\* \* \*

The little puppies had all turned as their
mother left and were making their way
over to the edges of the box.

All eight of them were wiggling and bouncing on the
floor and they looked so wonderful she couldn't

imagine ever leaving them. A smile appeared on her face when both her and Matthew reached down and picked one up. Hers had been the one she liked last time. A lovely little girl who was a little darker, almost sandy colored, than the others. Once more she squirmed in her hands as if she wanted to be closer to her.

It was such a wonderful feeling she didn't notice the tears that ran down her face.

She could picture herself working in a pet store, surrounded by puppies, and other animals, all day long. Maybe that should be her purpose. Maybe that was what God wanted her to do. Taking care of animals was a very rewarding job and they were always so eager to please. One of the best things that she loved about animals was their loyalty. They never turned their backs on their owners or the people that they loved. Dogs were loyal to the core, unlike people, they didn't care what you looked like, and this was why she had always wanted one.

"Aren't they precious?" Matthew asked. "They make me feel so full of love.

He surveyed the little ones jumping on and over each other.

"They are a rambunctious little bunch, aren't they?" he asked. Two of the puppies started play fighting and biting each other. One of the two wrestled his brother to the ground, and another one came charging in knocking them both over.

Gloria chuckled in delight. She could watch them play for the rest of her life. She would be the happiest she had ever been if she could stay in this room forever. But, she knew that was wishful thinking. She actually had to get back to running her errands before the day was over. She had a lot of work that needed to be accomplished.

She put down the sandy colored puppy and watched it run at its littermates. Within a few seconds she turned and ran back to Gloria and pawing her the box for her to pick him up again.

"I think that one really likes you," Matthew said.

"You think so?" Gloria asked. She picked her up and the puppy started licking her face.

"Yes, I think she likes you," Matthew said as he watched the other puppies playing around.

Feeling the little creature as it even licked her scar, she knew that she was falling in love. It was so wonderful to hold the bundle of joy and know that it would never judge her. If she took her home she would love her. She knew she had fallen in love only it made her heartbreak knowing that she couldn't take this one home with her. So, she stalled and let her play with her for as long as everyone in the room would allow.

"Out of all the puppies in the litter, this is the one that has decided to choose you as her owner. I think that you should take this one home. She is never going to be the same without you. I don't think that she's going to ever forget you," Matthew said when he realized that she still hadn't put that particular puppy down.

"I would love too, but my father is allergic to dogs and I can't bring one over to the *haus*. I have always had a huge love for them, but I have to admire them from afar," she said lowering her head to hide the tears that threatened to fall.

"Oh, I had no idea."

"Yea, it's so bad that I'm going to have to wash my hands before I walk in the door so that I do not spread dog hair everywhere. I've been warned that he's very allergic," Gloria said.

"I am so sorry to hear that," he said as the puppy moved closer and tried to bite him playfully. "Well, if you can't have this little one, do you think that I could take her home? If not, is there another one that you would choose for me?" he asked.

Gloria looked around the room at all of the puppies and even though they were all cute, they didn't fit Matthew's personality. This puppy was a happy go lucky, playful thing and she didn't want to leave her with the rest.

"No, I think that you should take this one home. She has already taken to both of us and it would be wrong to make her have to go through the choosing process all over again. I mean, what would it do to her self-esteem to be turned down?" she asked with a smile.

"I agree with you. I think that she is the one that I will take home and raise as my very own. I don't

SARAH MILLER

want her to think badly of herself either," he chuckled.

"Well, it's settled. Let's go find Mrs. Thompson and tell her that you have picked one of the puppies from the bunch," Gloria said.

"Wait, I think that we should name her first. Would you do the honors?"

"You want me to name her?" she asked, her heart pounding as he looked her in the eyes.

He nodded in response.

Gloria looked the puppy up and down. She held her out to check out her glistening coat and that was when it hit her. "Sandy. I think that you should call her Sandy."

Matthew took the puppy out of Gloria's arms and held her up close. "Sandy is a good name for a dog. What do you think little one? Do you like the name Sandy?" he asked his new puppy. She yipped in reply.

"Have you two chosen any of the puppies yet? I have others who are interested in seeing them too," Mrs. Thompson said as she came back inside the room.

"I would like to take this one home," Matthew said as he held up Sandy.

"She will be greatly missed, but I know that you will give her a very good and decent home," she said. "With your parents gone, I know that she will also fill some of the loneliness that you still harbor in your heart from losing them."

"*Denke*," Matthew said in response to Mrs. Thompson's comment. She showed the two out the door, while she went back to show some other people the rest of the litter.

# CHAPTER EIGHT

*6 Humble yourselves, therefore, under God's mighty hand, that he may lift you up in due time. 7 Cast all your anxiety on him because he cares for you.*

*1 Peter 5: 6-7*

She watched Matthew turning away to head back to his farmhouse with the puppy tucked under his arm.

"You should come over and visit sometime, for Sandy's sake. She is going to miss you an awful lot," he said over his shoulder.

Gloria didn't know what to make of his statement. Was he trying a manipulation tactic on her again?

"I will do my best to find some time," she told him before she hurried off to complete the rest of her errands for the day. She knew that she had gotten sidetracked from the day's tasks because of the puppies. Now that she had come over and seen them, it was time to go and complete her business of the day.

*That Matthew thinks he is so funny.* She chuckled to herself. She would not feed into his little mind games. She knew that he had taken the time to ask her for help on choosing a puppy because he wanted to get into her good graces. She knew that he still had an agenda and she was not falling for it this time.

Still thinking of ways to rebut his advances she walked into the General Store and picked up some quilting supplies that she was running low on. Now that she had seen the new golden Labrador puppies, she had an idea that would make her Labrador quilt stand out from the rest of the other quilts she had been working on.

By the time that Gloria had finished all of her errands, the sun had moved high in the sky and she was famished. It was afternoon and she needed to go home and make something for the afternoon meal. When she got back to the *haus*, she expected her parents and sister to already be in the kitchen making something, but she was all alone. She put all of her parcels down, washed her hands and started to make a little sandwich.

She couldn't get Sandy's image out of her mind and before she knew it she had gotten up from her chair and had started to whip up a batch of blueberry muffins as an excuse to take over to Matthew's *haus* for him being so kind to her. This way she could go over there and play with the puppy.

MATTHEW HEARD a loud knock at the door. He was curious on who it was because he was not expecting any company today. He opened the door and much to his surprise, Gloria was standing on the other side of it.

"Gloria, what a pleasant surprise. Please come in," he said as he opened the door for her.

She walked in, holding the basket on her arm.

"What do I owe the visit?" he asked.

"I was at home making some blueberry muffins and I had quite a few extra. So, I thought that I would come down and bring you some muffins, as well as see how the newest member of your *haus* is getting on," she said.

"*Denke*," he said as he took the basket of muffins from her and sat them down on the kitchen table.

He then led her back into the living room and gestured for her to sit down.

"Things have been going great over here. After we left Mrs. Thompson's, we went to the store and I bought some necessities for Sandy, especially to help with *haus* training," he said.

Gloria looked around the room and noticed the new doggy bed, bowl and puppy pad just outside the back door. "What is that for?" she asked.

"That is to help her potty train. I don't want her going inside the house. This is supposed to be a very effective method," he told her.

When Sandy heard the sound of Gloria's voice she perked up and ran over to her.

"She must have missed you," Matthew said.

"I guess she did." Gloria got down on the floor and started to play with Sandy.

"I'm going to go and grab some refreshments," Matthew said. He headed into the kitchen and grabbed some *kaffe,* cups and the muffins. He put the muffins on a plate and brought everything out into the living room.

"*Denke,*" Gloria said as she took a cup from him.

He watched her play with Sandy for a few moments. The dog really took to her. He picked up one of the muffins and took a bite.

"This is good," he said to Gloria. The taste of the muffin brought tears to his eyes because it almost tasted like the ones his *mamm* made when he was a boy.

"*Denke,*" she said back.

"Sandy is going to be a very loved and well taken care of dog. When I heard that Mrs. Thompson's dog had puppies, I decided to go over and have a look. It has been very quiet and lonely over here since my parents died and I figured that a puppy would help me get through the pain of the loneliness," he said to her.

Gloria hadn't realized that Matthew was that lonely after his parent's death. She had assumed that he was happy out here on his own.

"Oh, I didn't realize that things were that hard on you out here. I need to apologize for assuming that you are fine. I never really asked you how you were doing after your parents passing."

Matthew sighed. This was a tough question for him to answer. There were days when things were fine, and he could get out of bed and complete his chores with no issue. Then there were other days where he had the hardest time getting out of bed, or his body would automatically walk into his parents' room to check on them and there was no one there.

"Things can be difficult at times, but I have found a way to manage. I think that Sandy will be good for me. She is a sweet and attentive dog, and since she is so little, I have to find the time to train her and take care of her more than if she was a bigger dog."

Gloria realized that that was very true. Matthew would give Sandy all of the attention that she deserves because he was lonely too and they both deserve to be loved. After talking to him for a little bit over an hour, she came to realize that Matthew was a really sweet man and that she had enjoyed their conversation together, which was something that was new to her.

CHAPTER NINE

*8 Be alert and of sober mind. Your enemy the devil prowls around like a roaring lion looking for someone to devour. 9 Resist him, standing firm in the faith, because you know that the family of believers throughout the world is undergoing the same kind of sufferings.*

*1 Peter 5: 8-9*

*G*loria had found every excuse she could think of for the past couple of weeks to go to Matthew's and spend time with Sandy.

Sandy had been growing fast and she was really

smart. She listened to Matthew really well and he said that she was probably better trained than any dog that was taken to obedience school.

That afternoon she had decided to go over there because they had eaten steaks for dinner the night before and she had kept all of the raw bones for her to chew on. She knew that the bones were good for her teeth. So she had wrapped them up and put them in a basket filled with new dog toys for her to enjoy as well.

Matthew had said that she spoiled Sandy too much, but she never had a dog that she could treat as her own. So, she considered this to be the next best thing.

"*Gut* afternoon, Matthew," Gloria said as she approached them in the barn.

Matthew had felt that it would be easier to train Sandy in an outside space. He gave her a lot of time and space to roam around the grounds in order to get familiar with her new home.

"*Gut* afternoon to you Gloria. What do you have there?" he indicated the basket that was hanging off of her arm with a big wide smile that made her stomach do a little flip.

"I brought some goodies for Sandy," she said as she pulled out four steak bones and some of the toys from her basket. Sandy must have been able to smell the bones because she ran over to Gloria and got excited like she was going to be fed. Gloria watched Matthew for instructions before she did anything. He was Sandy's master and she had to make sure that she was okay with that.

"Go ahead," he said with a smirk.

Gloria bent down and gave Sandy one of the bones. She graciously took the bone out of her hand and ran off to a nearby tree where she lay down in the shade and began to gnaw on her treat.

Matthew giggled and asked her if she would like to come inside for some refreshments.

Gloria followed him inside the house and sat down at the table while he prepared them some sandwiches and poured two glasses of fresh squeezed lemonade.

The two were soon talking, but Gloria could tell that there was something going on with Matthew. He was a little awkward today and more shy than usual. She didn't know what was up with him. But, she pushed it aside. Maybe she was just reading into things.

She thanked him for the plate that he sat in front of her and then the two continued to eat. Where there used to be laughter and joy, she noticed that he was uncomfortable.

"Matthew, is everything all right? You aren't acting like yourself," she said to him.

He put down his napkin and cleared his throat before talking. "This is really hard for me to bring up because I don't know how you are going to react, but I have been thinking and praying about this for a really long time," he said.

Gloria nodded and waited for him to continue.

"I really want to invite you to service. But, I don't dare to because of how you reacted to me the first time I asked if I could drive you home. I don't think that I could handle that rejection again," he said to her.

Gloria knew that he was really being honest about his feelings, and since she had spent some time with him, she felt that she could be honest with him without any judgments or backlash about what she felt.

"I understand how you feel. I just have a concern of my own. I don't want to be forced into a marriage through pity. All my life people have either been mean to me or they have treated me with false kindness because they felt sorry for what happened to me," she said as her hand automatically went up to her scar.

"I would love to live in a world where people were genuine about their feelings. I know that what I went through as a child was horrible, and even reprehensible, but that doesn't mean I need to be reminded of it every single day of my life."

"Gloria, no one has ever walked up to me and asked to speak to me about a possible courtship or marriage. I want you to know that from the beginning. Since we were kids, I have always found you pretty, and quite frankly, I have always admired your courage as well. Kids can be cruel at times, and I know that after the fire, when you came back with the scar on your face, people didn't know how to react to you. They thought somehow, they needed to treat you different and they did. They didn't understand that you never wanted to be treated any different. You wanted everyone to act like nothing had changed. Even though it had. Life as a child must have been very hard for you, but every time I think back I remember a strong, courageous girl who never let those bullies get in her way of living. That was one of the most beautiful things I have ever seen, and one of the things that I greatly admired about you. You are a very strong and beautiful woman, and I am glad that I have gotten to know you better in the last couple of weeks," Matthew ended the conversation nervously.

Gloria felt her eyes fill with tears but she raised her head. "*Denke,* I would love to go to service with you."

CHAPTER TEN

*10 And the God of all grace, who called you to his
eternal glory in Christ, after you have suffered a little
while, will himself restore you and make you
strong, firm and steadfast. 11 To him be the power
forever and ever. Amen.*

*1 Peter 5: 10-11*

Gloria waited for Matthew's buggy to stop in front of her *haus*. The other day when she was sitting inside Matthew's kitchen she had agreed to go to service with him this week.

He had made her feel like she was something special

that day. He had told her that he had always found her pretty and that he admired her for her courage. No one had ever told her anything like that before. And, it made her feel like he genuinely wanted to get to know her, and that he was not asking to take her to service out of pity.

Matthew's buggy stopped right in front of her parent's home and he jumped out to hold the door open for her. She smiled as she got in because she had never been treated like this before.

"*Gut* morning, Gloria. How are you on this lovely day?" he asked her.

"I am well today. How are you?" she asked.

"I am the same," he responded.

They both sat in comfortable silence until they reached the service hall. They had been spending quite some time together that it wasn't awkward to sit in silence.

Matthew helped her down from the buggy and heads turned in their direction when people noticed that they had come together. Gloria noticed a few smiles and a few glares, but she tended to ignore them because for some reason what they thought didn't seem to bother her today. This bought a bigger smile to her face and she seemed to carry herself with a little bit more confidence than she was used to. The couple parted ways and Gloria went to find her family over in the women's section.

She could feel Matthew's eyes on her during the service and this time it did not anger or agitate her. Instead she felt pretty. For the first time in her life, her hand did not go to her face to cover her scar. She left her face exposed for the whole congregation to see, and that did not bother her because Matthew actually found her attractive with her scars and for some reason they no longer left her feeling ashamed. She didn't necessarily need to go and hide them from anyone, including herself. She was Gloria, scars and all.

"Gᴜᴛ ᴍᴏʀɴɪɴɢ," Rebecca said to Gloria's *mamm* after service ended.

"*Gut* morning, niece," she answered back. "Gloria, this is the cousin that I had told you about. This is the one that has requested that I specifically help with her wedding."

Gloria nodded to her cousin in greeting and felt a huge lump start to form in her throat. This was the cousin that her parents had defended when she accused them of conspiring to plan a wedding behind her back. They were planning a wedding, it just wasn't hers. She had started to feel guilty after that day, especially when she realized that she had treated her parents unfairly. She had tried to justify her actions by telling herself that they didn't seem to understand what she was going through and how people treated her. She was tired of people pitying her and she would not marry for pity either.

After she had started spending so much time with Matthew, she realized that she had become an angry person. She was angry at the world for how it treated her. But, that really wasn't fair. Especially when it came to her parents because they have always been there for her and never treated her any differently.

"*Mamm,* can I speak to you for a moment?" she asked while they excused themselves from the group.

"Yes, of course my *dochder,* I always have time for

you. Now what did you need Gloria?" she asked her daughter.

Gloria sighed before she spoke. "I wanted to start by apologizing to you. I have not been fair to you or *daed* about the marriage conversation that I overheard a couple of weeks ago. I have been holding back a lot of animosity toward the community because of how they treat me, and I thought that I was past that. However, I ended up judging you all and calling you liars. I made this whole wedding about me and it has nothing to do with me," Gloria said.

"That is very mature of you to say, Gloria. I accept your apology and I know that your *daed* will as well. I understand that life has not been easy for you since the fire, but we have always tried to show you that your scars make you who you are. We cannot change how other people think or treat us, but we can change how we react to it. I have noticed that you have been spending quite some time with Matthew, and before you say anything, I am not pushing you in any way. However, I see the change in you since you two have become friends and it is a good change. You have started to be less angry with the world and started to accept yourself for who you are, scars and all," her *mamm* said as she walked back to the group of people.

Gloria followed behind her, and she thought about what her *mamm* said. She was proud of her because she had started to embrace parts of herself that she was ashamed about before.

THIS WAS the big day for Matthew. He had been spending a lot of time with Gloria for a few months now. They had been training Sandy together on the farm, and she had even accompanied him to service. He valued their time together and he felt like he never wanted it to end. He had been asking *Gott* to help him see where he needed to move forward in his life and it always kept going back to Gloria. He didn't seem to ever remember a time when he was that comfortable or happy in his life. He felt a comfortable happiness with his parents, but this was different. When he was with Gloria he felt pure bliss and he never wanted it to end.

The other day after service he had told Gloria that he wanted to meet her at the park on Tuesday. He thought that it would be a good idea if they took

Sandy out of her element and saw how she reacted to her training. Sandy had been a farm dog since the day she was brought home from the Thompson's. She didn't go anywhere off the property unless it was to the vet. Matthew felt that it was important for her to get comfortable with her surroundings, especially when they were training. They felt that it was imperative to do that before they brought her to a new surrounding where things were very unfamiliar to her. Today would be the test to see how she would react to her training at someplace new.

Gloria had met him at his *haus* and they had driven the buggy over together with Sandy. What Gloria did not know was that Matthew had prepared a romantic picnic lunch for the two of them. He had set everything up and then asked one of the community members if they would watch the area to make sure that no one would disturb it before they arrived.

"I have never been to this side of the park before," Gloria said while looking around. She had Sandy on a very short leash. This way Sandy would be able to smell her new surroundings, but it still left Gloria in control.

"Yes, there is a lake on the other side and I thought that it would be a nice change of scenery from what we are normally used to," he said nervously. He waited to hear if Gloria was going to say anything in regard to his response, but she didn't.

The two continued to walk, until they ran into his friend Harold, who gave them a little nod and then was on his way. Everything was exactly how he had left it

Gloria gasped in surprise.

Matthew had decorated one of the picnic tables with a blue and white checkered tablecloth. There were two place settings set up with two pewter plates, cups and silverware. A jug of fresh lemonade was set in front of a basket that must have contained their lunch.

"Matthew, what is all of this?" she asked him.

"I felt that we have been spending a lot of time together and that I wanted to do something special for you. I hope you don't mind," he responded to her.

She shook her head to tell him no, but he knew that she was at a loss for words.

"Please sit," he said as he grabbed Sandy's leash from her and tied it around the bench so that she couldn't run away and get in any trouble. He had even thought of the dog. There was a bone, a bowl of water and another with dog food to keep Sandy busy while they had their picnic.

"What did you bring for us?" she asked him.

Matthew opened the top of the basket and pulled out cold fried chicken, biscuits and homemade potato salad with fruit for dessert. He served the both of them and they both sat down to eat in silence.

"How is it?" he asked her.

She swallowed what was in her mouth before she responded. "The chicken is delicious. How did you learn to make it like this?" she asked.

"Can I tell you a little secret?"

Gloria nodded.

"I asked your *mamm* to help me with the food, and your *daed* gave his permission for the rest," he said.

"What do you mean the rest?"

Before Matthew could answer her. He stood up and

walked over to her. He sat down beside her and took her hand in his.

"Gloria, since I can remember I have always admired you for your unique beauty and courage. The last few months have made me the happiest I have been in my entire life, which is something I never thought I would have. Happiness didn't live in my *haus* growing up. My parents were sickly, and I had to take care of them from a very young age. That left me with no thought of my future. Now that they are gone, I have found that I didn't know where my future lay until *Gott* brought me to you. I know that this is the path that He wants me to take for my future and I believe this is the path He wants you to take as well. So, Gloria, I humbly ask you today, would you make me the happiest man and be my *fraa*?"

Her eyes filled with tears the moment he got the words out. "*Jah*, Matthew. I will marry you because I see how much you love me and that that love is genuine," she said in response.

## EPILOGUE

*12 With the help of Silas, whom I regard as a faithful brother, I have written to you briefly, encouraging you and testifying that this is the true grace of God. Stand fast in it.*

*13 She who is in Babylon, chosen together with you, sends you her greetings, and so does my son Mark. 14 Greet one another with a kiss of love. Peace to all of you who are in Christ.*

*1 Peter 5: 12-13*

* * *

"I can't believe she is forty pounds already and she is still a puppy," Gloria said to her husband, Matthew.

"I can't believe that six months ago, I proposed to you right here in this exact spot and now we are walking through here as a family," Matthew said in response.

Gloria looked around and smiled. This place held a particular memory of the second most important and special day of her life. The day she realized that she wanted to be a *fraa* and have a family of her own; even if it was just her, Matthew and Sandy for now. She would be happy with that outcome for the rest of her life. She wasn't a spring chicken and she didn't know if she was too old to have a child of her own.

Gloria bent over and almost threw up. The nausea came upon her out of nowhere.

Sandy whined and laid down waiting for her owner to come back up feeling okay.

"Are you all right?" Matthew asked Gloria.

"I will be once the nausea passes," she told him.

He sweetly took the leash out of her hand and put his hand on her back. He rubbed it back and forth to help break up whatever was causing her to feel sick.

"Why don't you sit down for a moment and have a sip of water?" he handed her a water bottle that he carried in his pocket and she sat down for a few moments until the nausea subsided.

She didn't really seem to understand what was going on with her. She didn't normally get sick and if she was sick it never happened like this. She had felt these waves of nausea three times this week and they came and went as quickly as they could. They didn't arrive with a fever or any other symptom. She could be doing just about anything and all of a sudden, she just felt the sudden urge to throw up. It was not a very comfortable feeling and if it continued to persist, she was going to have to make an appointment with one of the doctors in the community.

Matthew sat down beside her and took her hand in his. He wasn't one for affection, but he knew that his wife was feeling sick and he wanted to be there for her.

Sandy laid down in the grass and waited for her two owners to move.

"I know that we never talked about this because we are content with our little family," Matthew said.

Gloria turned her head in his direction.

"How would you feel about having a *boppli*?" he asked her.

"That is an odd question to ask a woman. Wouldn't that be a question that I would ask you at some point in time?"

Matthew laughed.

"Yes, I suppose it should be, but humor me at least," he said.

"Okay, I haven't given it much thought, but I think that I would like to have a *boppli* sometime in the future. It would be nice to expand our little family," she said.

"I agree. I think that having a family with you would be another great thing to add to the list. I don't know how much happier I can get, but I would love to find out," he said.

"Matthew, why did you ask me how I would feel about having a *boppli*?"

"Well, I have been sitting here thinking that you have had bouts of nausea for the last few days, three times this week to be exact. So, correct me if I'm wrong, but these bouts of nausea do not come from eating a type of food, lack of hydration, or come after a fever, correct?" he asked her.

"No, they do not. They don't seem to be caused by anything that I can explain, and they come at the weirdest times too," she said.

"Gloria, after giving it some thought, I think that you might be pregnant," he said.

Gloria's face paled. She didn't think of herself being much of a mother and now that she might actually be one, she was happy and scared all at the same time.

"What do we do in this instance? I can't believe that I could possibly be pregnant," she told her husband.

Matthew smiled back at her. He thought the happiest day of his life was when she agreed to marry him, right in this very same spot. And now they find out that they could be having a *boppli*. He felt like this place, the place they were sitting at, was sacred because important things always seemed to happen when they were in that particular spot.

"I think that our next step would be to pay a visit to the midwife. She can answer our questions and tell you if you are pregnant or not. This will ease our minds and not keep us wondering," he said.

Gloria agreed and they both decided to walk back to the buggy and take a drive over to the Midwives house. Here she would be able to tell her what was going on with them.

Matthew helped Gloria into the buggy and set Sandy down next to her. Sandy laid down on the bench and put her head down on her lap.

Gloria rubbed the top of Sandy's head and started to think about all of the possibilities that a new *boppli* would bring to their lives. New babies bring new adventures, personalities and love. Here would be a genuine being that would love her for who she was, scars or not. This little one would look at Gloria as her *mamm* and not too much could break the bond of a mother and her child.

She sat back in her seat and started imagining picnics in the park with one or two children: a boy and a girl. She started thinking about Matthew playing tag football or regular football with his son out in the field. She could picture the two boys running together, trying to get the ball and having a really good time. Watching the two of them together would make her so proud and if her pregnancy was true then she would be excited to watch her husband and child playing together in their front yard.

"I think that this could be a blessing for us," Matthew said as he pulled up to the midwife's house.

"I agree with you but remember that *boppli's* also bring change and that is not necessarily good or bad," she said.

"Don't worry about that. Whatever happens, if you are pregnant or not, this child will be loved and he or she will make us stronger as a family. I believe that. I believe that we will be able to take on anything that *Gott* throws us. And I am really happy to be able to introduce myself as a *daed*," he said with a wink.

Gloria took her husband's hand as the two of them walked into the waiting room to speak to the midwife about the new adventure that awaited them.

IF YOU ENJOYED this book you will love A Miracle Baby for the Amish Midwife.

The *boppli* took her first breath in the world and screamed. Emma chuckled as she handed her to her *mamm* for the first time. Ruth cooed as she took the miracle in her arms.

"She is so precious," Ruth said to Emma. "*Denke* for witnessing this birth. I don't think that I would have been able to get through it on my own."

"You are very welcome. I'm happy that everything went well. I am going to leave some herbs for you to use for healing, and I will come back and check up on you in a couple of days. But, if you need anything until then, please send someone to fetch me." Emily grabbed her basket and was about to leave when

Ruth's older son Henry came running inside the *haus*.

"Emma, *gut* I caught you," Henry said.

"Oh, Henry. You should meet your new *Schweschder*. Your *mamm* is resting in the other room, but she would be so grateful to see you."

"*Denke* Emma. But, I have just come from Bishop Belier's and I have some news for you. Please sit down." Emma put her basket back on the sofa and sat down next to Henry.

"What is it?" she asked. He hadn't even acknowledged what she had just said and that sent a curl of worry through her.

"There has been a terrible accident on your farm. By the time his field hand came to get some men to help, he didn't make it. I'm so sorry, Emma." Henry put his hand on her shoulder for comfort.

Emma gasped in horror, could he really mean... Her heart fell in her chest, and she grabbed it to hold herself together. It felt like the ground had been pulled out from underneath her.

The door to the back room opened and Roger walked

out of the room quietly. "They both are sleeping," he said. "Emma, I can't – what's the matter?" he asked when he saw the look on both faces of the people in the room.

"Aaron was killed in a farm accident this afternoon," Henry said sadly.

"Emma, I'm so sorry. Let me get you home. Son, listen out for your *m*amm. I'll be back in a little bit." He grabbed Emma's arm and helped her up from the sofa, taking the basket in his other arm, he led her out to the door and into the buggy.

Emma didn't really pay attention to how she got into the buggy or how she got home for that matter. When the initial shock had passed, she realized that she was sitting at home in her chair, drinking a cup of *kaffe*.

Her *mamm* was in the kitchen and other *familye* members were in the *haus* getting the table ready for dinner.

"Emma? Emma? Would you like to join us for dinner?" her *daed* asked her. Her *familye* must have come over when she was still in shock, yet she had no recollection of them arriving.

Emma nodded her head in approval and he took her arm and led her to the table. She wasn't used to not helping the others with dinner and she tried to get up to do something to help them.

"You don't need to do anything dear. You've had a very traumatizing day. Just sit down here and let us take care of you tonight," her *mamm* said as she set down a bowl of potatoes and gravy on the table. Everyone took their place around her and her brother said the mealtime prayer.

"Our kind, righteous, eternal heavenly father. We come before you this evening hour. *Denke* for our many blessings. *Denke* for bringing us together to be there for Emma in her time of need. Please bless the food that is set before us, and the hands that have prepared it. In Jesus name we pray. Amen."

The dishes were passed around the table, and Emma took the time to go through her thoughts. As she graciously put food on her plate, she started to put together the events of the day. As she looked around the table, it surprised her to know that her Aaron wasn't there, but she didn't really feel what she thought she was supposed to feel.

She had been married to her husband Aaron for quite a few years and they were never able to conceive a child. She had helped so many women deliver their own *boppli's* but she never had the experience of having her own. She never knew what the problem was. Yet, Aaron had wanted to have *kinder* of his own and blamed her for not giving them to him. It had caused a huge rift in their marriage, and she had felt like the worst *fraa* in the world for not being able to give her husband what he really wanted.

The moment she heard that Aaron had died in a farm accident she had felt the initial shock and pain. When all of that wore off she realized that she didn't feel heartbroken. She actually felt a sense of relief because now he would no longer be able to blame her for their lack of *kinder*. She was filled with guilt for she knew that was a bad thing to feel, but she felt that way nonetheless.

For the first time that she could remember she was actually able to enjoy a dinner with her *familye* without feeling a sense of shame for what she could not do in her marriage. For the first time in a long time she was able to sit back and be a part of her community who cared about her, and not feel like an outsider. She knew that she would mourn her husband because he was a *gut* man and it was the right thing to do. However, when the time of mourning had passed, she was going to move on with her life and start enjoying what was left of her younger years. Maybe this was what *Gott* really intended for her and her journey in life.

Find out if Gott has a miracle in store for Emma in A Miracle Baby for the Amish Midwife and read for FREE on Kindle Unlimited

Amish Faith and Love volume 1 a 15 book box set.

Amish Love in Faith's Creek 8 Book Boxed Set
http://bit.ly/1MWqvw9

Amish Christmas Boxset – A Celebration of Faith a 10
book box set

Bonnets & Babies 8 book Box Set http://bit.ly/1SDDr1D

A Christmas Baby Miracle

The Amish Grandson

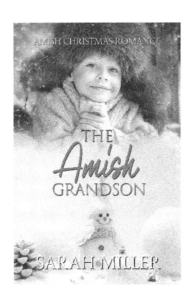

**Amish Hearts Return**

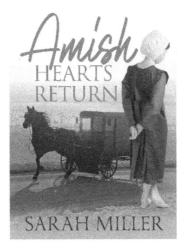

# An Amish Life and Love

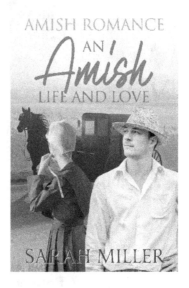

Sarah Miller is a Number One Bestselling Author of Amish Baby Hope, Amish in Faith's Creek, Amish Lost Love and many, many more.

She was born in Pennsylvania and spent her childhood close to the Amish people. Weekends were spent doing chores; quilting or eventually babysitting in the community. She grew up to love their culture and the simple lifestyle that they lead. She had many Amish friends. Sarah believes that the one thing that you can guarantee when you are near the Amish, is that you will feel close to God.

Many years later she married Martin who is the love of her life and moved to England. There she started to write stories about the Amish. Recently after a lot of persuasion from her best friend she has decided to publish her stories. They draw on inspiration from her relationship with the Amish and with God and she hopes you enjoy reading them as much as she did writing them. Many of the stories are based on true events but names have been changed and even though they are authentic at times artistic license has been used.

Sarah likes her stories to be simple and to hold a message and they help bring her closer to her faith. She currently lives in Yorkshire, England with her husband Martin and seven very spoiled chickens.

She would love to meet you on facebook at https://www.facebook.com/SarahMillerBooks

Sarah hopes her stories will both entertain and inspire and she wishes that you go with God.

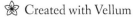 Created with Vellum

CPSIA information can be obtained
at www.ICGtesting.com
Printed in the USA
LVHW091047221020
669528LV00006B/179

9 781793 876744